This **ELMER** book belongs to:

. . . . . . . . . . . . . . . . . . .

# To Dominique and Nicky

This paperback edition first published in 2009 by Andersen Press Ltd.
First published in Great Britain in 2007 by Andersen Press Ltd.,
20 Vauxhall Bridge Road, London SW1V 2SA.
Copyright © David McKee, 2007
The rights of David McKee to be identified as the author and illustrator
of this work have been asserted by him in accordance with the
Copyright, Designs and Patents Act, 1988.
All rights reserved.
Colour separated in Switzerland by Photolitho AG, Zürich.
Printed and bound in China.

10    9    8    7    6    5    4

British Library Cataloguing in Publication Data available.

ISBN 978 1 84270 716 6

# David McKee

# ELMER
## and the Rainbow

Andersen Press

Elmer, the patchwork elephant, was in a cave, sheltering from a storm. With him were other elephants and birds. "Thunder and lightning is exciting," said Elmer. "And after the storm we might see a rainbow."

When the storm had stopped,
Elmer and the birds went outside.
Elmer felt drops on his head.
"Oh," he said. "It's still raining!"
"Perhaps it's the rainbow crying,"
said a bird. "It's come out too soon
and lost its colours. Look!"

In the sky was a pale shape. "A rainbow without colours!" said Elmer. "That's awful. We must do something. I'll give it my colours."

"To do that you'll have to find where it touches the ground," said a bird. "Nobody knows where that is."

"Well, what are we waiting for?" said Elmer. "Let's start searching. You go that way and I'll go this."

"What are you looking for, Elmer?" called Lion.
"The end of the rainbow," said Elmer. "Have you seen it?"
"Which end?" asked Lion.
"Either end," said Elmer. "The rainbow's lost its colours. I can give it mine, if we can find the end."
"A rainbow without colours? That is serious," said Tiger. "Come on, Lion, we'd better search. You too, rabbits."
"We'll roar, when we find it," said Lion.

A little later Elmer met Giraffe. "Elmer," she said, "there's something strange in the sky."
"That's the rainbow," said Elmer and he told her about the lost colours. "Can you see where it touches the ground?" Giraffe stretched very high. "No, I can't," she said. "What will happen to you, Elmer, if you give it your colours?" she asked. But Elmer was already on his way to get the elephants.

The elephants were still in the cave. "We're not coming out with that thing in the sky," they said. But when Elmer had explained the problem, the elephants were keen to help.

"What about Elmer, if he gives his colours away?" asked an elephant.

"I suppose he'll be like us," said his friend.

"Better that than a colourless rainbow!"

Elmer was with the monkeys when the birds returned. "No luck so far," they said. "We'll keep looking."
"Nobody can find the end of the rainbow," said a monkey. "But it will be fun to try."

By the time Elmer arrived at the river, everyone was looking for the rainbow. "Hello, fish," he called. "I don't suppose you know where the rainbow starts, do you?"

"Usually at the waterfall," said a fish, "but today there's some pale thing there."

"That's the rainbow!" said Elmer. "Come on, to the waterfall!"

Sure enough, a colourless rainbow
was coming from the waterfall. The search
was over! Elmer, the fish and the crocodiles called
loudly to the other animals. Then, without waiting,
Elmer went behind the waterfall.

By the time the other animals arrived, Elmer was out of sight. Colours gradually began to appear in the rainbow.

"Hurrah!" cheered the animals.

"But what about Elmer?" whispered an elephant.

As if in answer, Elmer appeared from behind the waterfall.
He still had his colours! The animals cheered again.
"But Elmer," said an elephant, "you gave your colours to
the rainbow. How can you still have them?"
Elmer chuckled, "Some things you can give and give and
not lose any. Things like happiness or love or my colours."

Later, on the way home, Tiger said, "I wondered if the rainbow would be patchwork."
Elmer grinned.
"Don't even think about it," said Lion. "We have enough trouble with a patchwork elephant!"
This time Elmer laughed out loud.